J
PIC
VER

For my good friend Abby Parigian, unlike any other
—A.V.

To my own hoodie-and-glasses-wearing monster, Gabriel Jack. Love, Dad
—C.J.

Text copyright © 2016 by Audrey Vernick
Illustrations copyright © 2016 by Colin Jack

Printed in Malaysia
First Edition, July 2016
1 3 5 7 9 10 8 6 4 2
FAC-029191-16074

Library of Congress Cataloging-in-Publication Data

Vernick, Audrey.
  Unlike other monsters / by Audrey Vernick ; illustrated by Colin Jack.—First edition.
    pages cm
  Summary: "Zander is a monster. And monsters don't have friends. But one day Zander meets Bird,
and a strange thing happens. They start to spend some time together. Zander even tells Bird a secret no
one else knows about. When another monster asks, 'Is that your friend?' Zander says no . . . but is that
true?"—Provided by publisher.
  ISBN 978-1-4231-9959-5 (hardcover)
[1. Monsters—Fiction. 2. Birds—Fiction. 3. Friendship—Fiction.] I. Jack, Colin, illustrator. II. Title.
  PZ7.V5973Un 2016
  [E]—dc23   2015020225

Designed by Tyler Nevins
Text is set in Cheddar Salad
Art is created digitally using Adobe Photoshop
Reinforced binding

Visit www.DisneyBooks.com

Unlike Other MONSTERS

Written by **Audrey Vernick**

Illustrated by **Colin Jack**

DISNEP • HYPERION
Los Angeles   New York

Zander was a monster.
This wasn't strange, as
Zander's mother was a monster.
His father, too.

Oddly, his sister was a **fairy**.

And his dog was a **skunk**.

Like other monsters, Zander didn't have friends. When he passed a monster he knew, Zander lifted his chin in a way that meant, I know you. The other monster would chin-point back.

That's about how far it went, for monsters.

Zander's sister, Lilybelle, had friends.
It sort of went along with being a fairy.

Lilybelle's friends flitted
about Zander's home like
sparks of happiness.

Which was nice if you liked that kind of thing.

Zander did not.

Luckily, Zander didn't care about friends.

Like other monsters, he enjoyed scrapbooking,

raisin bread,

and showing up in
unexpected places
to scare children.

But more than anything,
Zander loved

SURFING.

There was **nothing** like
that moment on a wave:
power and joy,
peace and thrill,
water and flight.

Paddling out one day, Zander noticed something.

A bird was watching him.

Each time Zander peeked, there it was, watching.

What does it **want**? he wondered.

Who could tell, with birds?

While Zander was packing up,
the bird nod-nod-nodded at him.
Zander chin-pointed back.

The next day,
the same thing.

The day after that, too.

A day later, Zander smoothed a circle
in the sand next to him.

The bird landed in the center.

Other monsters noticed.

"Hey, Zander," Felix said,
"is that your **friend**?"

Monsters never spoke in long sentences, so
Zander was surprised when he wanted to say:
I don't really see how a bird could be my
friend, Felix, since monsters don't
have friends—it wouldn't be very
monsterlike at all, would it?

Instead, he just said, "No."

Did the bird look disappointed?

Who could tell, with birds?

The monsters walked off to their scrapbook meeting.
Zander knew their pages would all look alike,
because monsters did the same things.
But Zander didn't feel like doing the same old thing.

He felt something like a **hole** inside his monster self.

At home, he asked Lilybelle,
"What do you and your friends do?"

"We talk, eat, hang out."

"What else?"

"Share secrets. Give money to kids who've lost teeth."

It was a **lot** to remember.

The next day, Zander smoothed a circle in the sand, looked toward the sky, and waited. When the bird came back, he asked, "Are you looking for a friend?"
The bird nod-nod-nodded.

"You should meet Lilybelle," he said. "She has friends."

The bird just stared.

So Zander decided to tell the bird something he'd never told anyone.

"When I surf, I feel like I'm **flying**."

For the first time, the bird joined Zander on his board. She seemed a little wobbly. Nervous. Zander offered her a bit of raisin bread. She grabbed it in her beak and nod-nod-nodded at him. Zander chin-pointed back.

Other monsters noticed.

"Hey, Zander," Felix said,
"is that your **friend**?"

Zander thought about Lilybelle's list —
talk, eat, secrets, teeth, money.

WAIT!

He and the bird hadn't once given money
to a kid who had lost teeth.
Birds probably didn't even know what money was.
Or what teeth were. Was that a deal breaker?

Of course it was.

Everyone knew monsters didn't have friends.

The bird was just someone Zander
looked forward to seeing every morning.

Someone to chin-point at.

Someone who nodded back.

Someone to share food—and secrets—with.

Someone who understood the joy of flight.

Someone to say good-bye to,
knowing that tomorrow,
they would be **together** again.

Zander hoped **someday** he and the bird might find a way to give money to kids who lost teeth.

Until then, they spent their days together, walking the skunk, sharing raisin bread,

flying high
above the sea . . .

and scaring children by showing up
in really, really **unexpected** places.